STAR WARS®
KNIGHT ERRANT
AFLAME

VOLUME FIVE

SCRIPT
JOHN JACKSON MILLER

PENCILS
IVAN RODRIGUEZ

INKS
IVAN RODRIGUEZ
BELARDINO BRABO

COLORS
MICHAEL ATIYEH

LETTERING
MICHAEL HEISLER

COVER ART
JOE QUINONES

The innocent residents of Chelloa face destruction, thanks to the greed of the Sith. Earlier, Lord Odion tried to destroy the planet, denying his hated brother Daiman access to its underground veins of explosive baradium. Now, Odion returns on a new mission: to capture the planet and the mobile factories Daiman has landed there.

Chelloa's only hope, Kerra Holt, has only recently regained hope herself. Following an escalating series of suicidal attacks against the warring brothers, Kerra receives wise counsel from Gorlan Palladane, a former Jedi. She realizes her destiny isn't death, but life: finding a way to extricate the innocents from the battlefield.

Sensing that Daiman has a diabolical welcome planned for Odion, Kerra boldly declares her intent to bring *all* the residents offworld. An impossible job for a Jedi alone, but, as Gorlan says in taking up his lightsaber again, this time, she won't be alone . . .

This story takes place approximately 1,032 years BBY.

visit us at www.abdopublishing.com

Reinforced library bound edition published in 2012 by Spotlight,
a division of the ABDO Group, PO Box 398166, Minneapolis, MN 55439.
Spotlight produces high-quality reinforced library bound editions for schools and libraries.
Published by agreement with Dark Horse Comics, Inc., and Lucasfilm Ltd.

Printed in the United States of America, North Mankato, Minnesota.
102011
012012
This book contains at least 10% recycled materials.

Library of Congress Cataloging-in-Publication Data

Miller, John Jackson.
Star wars : knight errant. volume 1 Aflame / script, John Jackson Miller ; pencils, Federico Dallocchio. -- Reinforced library bound ed.
p. cm.
"Dark Horse."
"LucasFilm."
Summary: Eighteen-year-old Kerra Holt, a Jedi Knight on her first mission, is left deep in Sith space without any support or resources and realizes how unprepared she is, but will not abandon the Jedi's mission to help the colony.
ISBN 978-1-59961-986-6 (volume 1) -- ISBN 978-1-59961-987-3 (volume 2)
ISBN 978-1-59961-988-0 (volume 3) -- ISBN 978-1-59961-989-7 (volume 4)
ISBN 978-1-59961-990-3 (volume 5)
1. Graphic novels. [1. Graphic novels. 2. Science fiction.] I. Dallocchio, Federico, ill. II. Title. III. Title: Knight errant. IV. Title: Aflame.
PZ7.7.M535St 2012
741.5'973--dc23

2011031240

All Spotlight books are reinforced library binding
and manufactured in the United States of America.

"THE DELUDED SEE MORNING AS A BEGINNING--BUT I SEE IT FOR WHAT IT IS. AN ENDING, WAITING TO HAPPEN.
"EVERY LIVING THING IS BORN DYING. AND WHEN DEATH DOESN'T COME FAST ENOUGH--
"--I STEP IN."
THIS IS THE PLACE! I CAN FEEL THE DESTRUCTION YET TO COME!
LORD ODION! DESTROY HIM!
"MY POWER TEMPTS MY ENEMIES TO THROW THEMSELVES INTO THE FIRE. I ONLY WISH THERE WERE MORE OF THEM HERE.
"I WILL NEVER KNOW PEACE WHILE OTHER BEINGS EXIST--

"-- AND I HAVE SO MUCH WORK TO DO."
LIGHTNING GUARD -- ATTACK!
HOLD YOUR GROUND, DAIMANITES! YOUR TRUE LORD COMMANDS!

THERE ARE YOUR OBJECTIVES--
--THOSE PYRAMIDS HOLDING THE MOBILE MUNITIONS PLANTS! TAKE THEM INTACT--I CAN USE THEM!
I CAN SENSE THE DEATHS THEY'LL CAUSE. SO MANY--
--SO WONDERFUL.

HIDE ON YOUR MOUNTAIN, BABY BROTHER! I'LL TAKE EVERYTHING ELSE!
SO PREDICTABLE, "BROTHER"--
--YOUR IDEA OF SURPRISE IS PUNCHING WITH YOUR LEFT HAND INSTEAD OF YOUR RIGHT.
YOU WERE RIGHT, LORD DAIMAN--
--ODION'S BROUGHT HIS ENTIRE LIGHTNING GUARD! THEY'VE FALLEN FOR YOUR TRAP!
OF COURSE. I GAVE THEM EYES SO THEY COULD SEE--
--EXACTLY WHAT I WANTED THEM TO SEE. I'VE GIVEN EVERY INDICATION I INTEND TO EXPLOIT CHELLOA--
--EVEN CONVINCING THAT SILLY JEDI.
AND I WILL EXPLOIT IT--
--NOW. FACTORY CARRIER UNITS--DEPLOY!

ALL UNITS NOW CONVERGING ON THE FACTORIES, MY LORD! WE'LL CAPTURE ALL TEN, EASY!
IT'S ALMOST *TOO* EASY!
THESE AREN'T DAIMAN'S BEST TROOPS AT ALL! I KNOW CANNON FODDER WHEN I GUT IT!
JUST LIKE WITH THE TOKEN RESISTANCE IN ORBIT -- HE'S LET US ADVANCE TOO FAR, TOO FAST! BUT WHY WOULD HE --
LORD ODION! LOOK THERE! THE PYRAMIDS --
KRRRAAAANNNNG
-- *THEY'RE OPENING!*
THAT'S -- THAT'S NOT A MUNITIONS FACTORY! THAT'S --

--THAT'S A KINETIC CORRUPTOR!
THEY'RE ALL KINETIC CORRUPTORS!

LITTLE SNOT STOLE MY IDEA!
THEY'RE ACTIVATING! WE'VE GOT TO GET OFF THE SURFACE, NOW!
VRRRMMMMM
THE GAME IS OVER. I WIN.
IT WAS ALWAYS THE DESTINY OF THIS PLANET TO DESTROY ODION --
"-- ONE WAY OR ANOTHER. BUT WHY BOTHER PUTTING BARADIUM INTO BOMBS? THE WHOLE PLANET CAN BE THE WEAPON!"
PREPARE MY SHUTTLE. AND ORDER THE DECOY TRANSPORTS PARKED BY THE TOWNS TO LIFT OFF. I'M ALREADY SACRIFICING CHELLOA --
-- NO NEED TO BE WASTEFUL!

FOOLS! COME BACK HERE!
RRRMMMBBLLL
YOU'LL NEVER REACH OUR LANDERS IN TIME! GO *TOWARD* THE CORRUPTORS -- AND DAIMAN'S *TRANSPORTS!*
SORRY, ODION --

--BUT THIS FLIGHT'S FULLY BOOKED. YOU'LL HAVE TO WAIT FOR THE NEXT ONE!
YOU! GET OUT OF THE WAY, JEDI! THIS DOESN'T CONCERN YOU!
SURE IT DOES. REMEMBER--
--THIS IS HOW WE MET! WE BOTH SKIPPED OUT BEFORE THE FIREWORKS, LAST TIME--
--YOU DON'T WANT TO MISS THEM AGAIN, DO YOU?

WHY ARE MY TRANSPORTS STILL ON THE GROUND? ODION COULD USE THEM TO ESCAPE!
WE'RE TRYING TO REACH THE CREWS, MY LORD! THEY SHOULD HAVE RECEIVED YOUR ORDER --BUT THEY'RE NOT RESPONDING!
GIVE ME THAT! I CAN'T TRUST YOU NONENTITIES WITH ANYTHING!
THERE. THE TRANSPORT NEAR ARBOTH. THERE'S GOT TO BE A REASON THEY HAVEN'T LEFT--
--PALLADANE?!

HURRY-- EVERYONE ABOARD! THIS PLANET'S ABOUT TO GIVE OUT ON US!
RRRMMBBLLL
ALL THE SHIPS HAVE REPORTED IN, GORLAN! YOUR AMBUSHES WORKED. THE VILLAGERS ARE IN CONTROL --AND LOADED UP!
LIFT OFF, ROAH --
--AND CALL KERRA'S TEAM! TELL HER WE'VE GOT EVERYONE THAT CAN WALK, HOBBLE, OR CRAWL! THE FREEDOM FLEET IS ON ITS WAY!
OH, AND IF YOU'RE WATCHING UP THERE, DAIMAN --
-- WE QUIT!

STOP THEM! SHOOT THEM DOWN! WHERE'S MY *DEFENSE FLEET?*
YOU CALLED IT AWAY, LORD, TO ALLOW ODION TO LAND! NOW *WE* HAVE TO GO BEFORE THE MOUNTAIN COLLAPSES!
I CREATED THIS MOUNTAIN! *IT WILL DO AS I SAY!*
YOU DID -- BUT IT'S NOT LISTENING *NOW!*

YOU CAN'T ESCAPE ME LIKE THIS!
APPARENTLY NOT--

-- HOW ABOUT LIKE THIS?
EH?
YAAAAHHHH!
KRANNGG!!

FACE ME! I COMMAND YOU!
LATER. I'M BUSY!

OOOOF!
THUD
YOU LEAP LIKE A GIZKA -- BUT YOU'VE RUN OUT OF PERCHES.
I SEE WHAT YOU'RE DOING. YOU'RE TRYING TO DIVERT ME FROM THE LIVING TRASH INSIDE THESE SHIPS.
BUT IT'S YOU THAT I WANT. YES. I REMEMBER YOUR PRESENCE NOW.
AQUILARIS, WASN'T IT? TEN YEARS AGO. SO MANY DEATHS -- I WISHED THAT DAY WOULD NEVER END.
BUT I WAS FORCED TO LEAVE BEFORE I FOUND EVERYONE -- AND I HATE TO LEAVE A JOB INCOMPLETE.
SO DO YOU. YOU'D GIVE YOUR LIFE TO STOP ME. SO DO IT!
TURN! DESTROY ME!

SORRY-- THAT'S NOT HER JOB.
A JEDI. I BROUGHT YOU TO CHELLOA--
WHO THE BLAZES ARE YOU?
--AND THIS IS WHERE YOU'RE GOING TO STAY!
THE GIRL FIRST, BEGGAR. WAIT YOUR TURN!
I'VE WAITED LONG ENOUGH!
GORLAN, NO!

FOOL! THE THRUSTERS-- YOU'LL KILL US BOTH!
THAT'S THE IDEA!
YAAARRGGHHH!

A LITTLE... TOO MUCH CABLE. VANNAR ALWAYS SAID --GIVE ME ENOUGH ROPE...
GORLAN, YOU DIDN'T HAVE TO DO THIS! YOU WERE FREE! YOU'D ESCAPED!
YOU WERE...DYING FOR THE WRONG THING...BUT I WAS LIVING FOR THE WRONG THING.
YOU'RE... LIKE ME, KERRA-- A KNIGHT ERRANT. WE MAY STRAY...BUT WE ALWAYS FIND THE RIGHT PATH.
DON'T WORRY -- I'LL GET YOUR PEOPLE BACK TO THE REPUBLIC.
THEY'RE YOUR PEOPLE NOW--
--AND THERE ARE BILLIONS MORE OUT HERE THAT NEED YOU. SAVE THEM, KERRA--
--COMPLETE YOUR MISSION...

THE SPIKE, DAYS LATER.
WORD FROM OUR SPIES, MY LORD! THE TRANSPORTS HAVE LEFT DAIMAN'S SPACE FOR THE REPUBLIC!
HIS VESSELS AND SLAVES HAVE BEEN DENIED HIM -- ALONG WITH THE BARADIUM OF CHELLOA! VICTORY IS YOURS!
YOU CALL THIS VICTORY, JELCHO? MY BEST LEGION'S GONE -- AND HALF MY ARMOR'S FUSED TO MY SKIN!
IF THAT JETPACK HADN'T GOTTEN ME TO ONE OF OUR TRANSPORTS, I'D HAVE JOINED THE VOID MYSELF!
MY LORD, PLEASE REMAIN STILL! WE'RE REMOVING WHAT WE CAN, BUT YOU'LL ONLY INCREASE THE PAIN --
I WANT THE PAIN! I WANT TO REMEMBER IT EVERY TIME I THINK OF VANNAR TREECE'S WHELP!

NILASH, A WORLD IN THE DAIMANATE.
AS MY LORD KNOWS, PRODUCTION HAS SUFFERED HERE AND ACROSS THE REALM --
-- WITHOUT THE EXPECTED BARADIUM FROM CHELLOA. IT'S MADE PRESSING OUR ADVANTAGE DIFFICULT.
A SMALL MATTER, ULEETA. WHAT'S IMPORTANT IS THE JEDI WOMAN IS GONE. I EXPECT SHE BURNED ON CHELLOA --
-- AND I'LL TRADE A FEW TRANSPORTS IF IT KEEPS WORD OF HER FROM GETTING OUT. I CAN'T ABIDE DISTRACTIONS.
THAT'S WHY THE ADMINISTRATOR HERE CALLED, MY CREATOR. SOMEONE ENTERED THE MUNITIONS PLANT AND FREED THE NATIVE WORKERS LAST NIGHT.
WE BELIEVE THE SLAVES SIMPLY MELTED BACK INTO THE JUNGLE.
NO AGENT OF ODION'S WOULD FREE SLAVES. WAS ANYTHING MISSING?
ONLY A SINGLE HIGH-POWERED LASER, MY LORD, DESIGNED FOR CUTTING CORTOSIS. IT'S HARD TO SEE THE STRATEGIC IMPORTANCE.
IT'S A MESSAGE.
TO ME.

SHE WANTS ME TO KNOW--SHE EXISTS.
SHE EXISTS--
"--AND SHE'S NOT GOING AWAY..."
THE END.